AF271711

A1DAY STORIES

By Vivaan Sadare

TABLE OF CONTENTS

INTRODUCTION

I know you cannot deny that at one stage or the other, especially during the pandemic, you've had thoughts (if not in-depth), fleeting thoughts of what to do to have a fun time with friends and families. Well, no worries, I've had those thoughts too. Having fun with friends and family is undeniably good therapy. But, besides the fact that it does so much to the mind and body, it is also a way of building and strengthening new and old relationships with those you love.

But things changed drastically in 2020.

As if the yearly dose of Hurricanes, floods, earthquakes, volcanoes, and such natural disasters were not enough, there was the terrible outbreak of a new virus. YIKES!

It damaged our lives (literally!) and disrupted our regular routines such that being indoors became the new normal. We were forced to include the unsolicited, discomforting, and unwanted piece of clothing into our lives- the "MASK." Whew, sorry about being so dramatic; it's just that me and my friends had a hard time adjusting to it.

The virus devastated many families and then HAD THE AUDACITY to mutate and send multiple variants our way. We barely had a chance to recover from the still looming deadly virus, and yet, a new WAR and energy crisis came along. It's always something. It now feels like we're living in fear because, at any moment, something new could pop up and could pull our mental health off balance.

We all know that these waves of disasters are a natural course of life, but no one knows what is coming next. However, for now, we have had enough of this seemingly unending cycle of negativity. We need a breath of fresh air; we need a break. We need positivity.

We need hope to face these challenges and a new set of masks (seriously, we're running out of them). Humor aside, though, who else has felt the need to boost their happiness lately?

As for me, I need it badly. I need some happiness every single day.

I know what it feels like to think that everything around you sucks and there isn't much you can do, and I also know what it feels like to desperately want to get out of the evil grasp of negativity. So ever since this virus started, I have come up with new ideas every day.

Trust me, I researched them, worked on them, experimented with them, and I kept my experiences flowing into my journal.

So, friends and folks, this is what this book is about. I am 'Dhoren.' Well, that is my last name, but that is what my friends call me. Sometimes they also call me by my nickname, which is D, as in "Hey, D," many around me call me by my last name (except family members, of course).

I would like to share my thoughts and tips to have an 'a1Day'.

The significant points are based on my experiences from these past few years, especially the lethal (as we know) pandemic years. How these experiments made me happy, and I would like you to try and check if they help you too.

Interested? If yes, read along.

Now, I will not tell you how to live your life, I know very well that is not my business, but I will give you my secrets to make life remarkably interesting (to say the least.) I will be sharing my stories and hope they help someone or maybe make a tiny bit of a difference in your day. So, let's get on to it.

I.

A Lousy Haircut won't stop me

I think that sometimes to make the most fun out of moments in your life, you must learn to ignore certain things. Note that I said IGNORE. This means that although we do not like it, it is inevitable to have ugly moments in our life. People are bound to say mean things; things are bound to go wrong, but you just have to close your eyes to them and only focus on the good stuff.

Ignorance connects us to something much more. It helps us see the bigger picture while filtering the unnecessaries. Ignorance gives us the power to select what we want in our lives and what we don't. Therefore, it all lies in your hands whether you allow positivity or negativity.

Once you have mastered the art of ignorance, you begin to see the fun!

I remember, mid pandemic, we were trying to avoid all the social contact we could and stay in the safety of our home. Our lives were on hold (for the most part); however, some things were not affected by the lockdown—for example, my hair. The lockdown did not stop my hair from growing.

Usually, we visit the salon every two months or so, but due to the prevailing circumstances, we kept postponing and waiting for things to open. I had not had a haircut in almost five months. My hair was long, and I was in dire need of a haircut, but salons in the area were not open. I started to get uncomfortable, so mom tried to improvise. She decided to give it a try at home.

Lucky for my dad, he had a haircut right before the shutdown and could live off haircuts longer than me for sure. So, I was the guinea pig.

We got all the supplies off amazon. Mom educated herself with online YouTube videos and decided to try them.

Boy, it turned out to be my biggest haircut pet peeve. First, it hurt because they were so long, I think we should have used scissors before the razor, but since it was her first time, she did not know that. Then, the pain started to get worse, and we weren't even anywhere near the end, so mom tried to quicken her pace. Apart from her even trying, this was another bad idea because the razor left uneven lengths.

The Bottom line, she could not do it right, and my hair ended up being a nightmare. It was shorter than my usual cut, uneven, and looked weird. It was very noticeable, but we weren't going out much anyway, so it was ok.

Or at least that's what I thought.

I carried on with my life normally and remained bothered about my hair until one evening. When I decided to leave the house to get a little bit of 'fresh air.'

I was out in the neighborhood playing with my bike on the sidewalk, and two other kids were also playing on scooters on the other side of the road. I had my bike helmet on, so they did not notice my hair. Everything was fine as we played separately. I got so carried away with playing that I forgot about the haircut.

When mom called me in for dinner, I took off my helmet, rested it on my bike's handle, and started walking my bike inside the garage. I heard a laugh. When I turned around quickly enough, I realized they were laughing at my haircut. I went in quickly, a little embarrassed, knowing full well they were going to spread the word about my haircut and have a few mean jokes about it.

The following day, I went with my dad to get the groceries. I tried hiding my bad haircut under my baseball cap to avoid such embarrassment, just in case. Luckily, we did not run into anyone at that time, as grocery stores were allowing a limited number of people in at a time. That same afternoon I was out in our driveway washing the car with my dad when I noticed those two kids again. I think they were making sidewalk chalk drawings on the other side of the street.

Somewhere in the middle of our washing, my dad went inside to get dry towels, and like they had been patiently waiting for an opportunity, one of them hollered at me. "Dude, you look like you got corona on your head."

I didn't know how to feel because it was funny and sad at the same time, so I just ignored it. I shook my head and laughed it off to hide my feelings.

When my dad came outside, he noticed my mood and guessed what may have happened. He is a playful person; he always brings laughter and happiness around him. He loves to make jokes.

He told me that day, "If you want to be happy, you have to make yourself immune to other people's comments and actions about you. People are nice but not all the time. Sometimes they say mean things. Ignore it or make a joke about it."

I had two choices. To simply ignore or continue letting their mean comments steal my happiness. When it comes to happiness, I believe it is a matter of choice, and the simple act of ignorance will do so much good. You can acquire freedom and save yourself a whole lot of stress by just being oblivious.

I know it can be tricky, especially when the source of the comment is hanging freely on your head. Literally!

I followed his advice, and on another occasion, when they made a similar comment, I responded by saying, "it's a new fashion, dude; keep up."

Once those kids realized that I wasn't bothered by their comments, they just stopped.

This is always the result when you choose to put your happiness first. When the negativity around you finally sees that you are unbothered by its presence, it flees. In a world where all the words, negativity, and hate come at you very fast, ignorance is sort of like having an invincible shield around you. Yes, these things come at you, but they won't touch you.

I got used to my hair, and it grew back in a few weeks. So this time, mom invited one of her friends to give me a private haircut at home. She lived a little far, but she ran her salon for a few years and had expertise in kids' hair. She fixed my hair in no time; it was a nice haircut.

Ultimately, fun is a state of mind and ignorance is the key to unleashing it. So don't depend on something to make you happy/or have fun. Yes, many things bring you fun, but only you can make yourself truly happy.

What I learned from this, though, do not let that negativity get to you. Stop giving negative things power over you. If you want to be happy, ignore the nasty comments.

2.

Biking = Free Donuts 🍩

Ok, this one is no secret. Being active can boost your productivity. I kid you not. Being active is essential for maintaining a healthy routine, especially during a pandemic. There are a lot of ways you can be active. Exercise is a common way. Basic exercises like squats, push-ups, and skipping are great ways to boost productivity. You can also be active by doing the things you enjoy like dancing, swimming, playing tennis, hiking, cycling, and even cooking!

Maybe actually cooking or just standing by your mother in the kitchen and helping out with a few things. Being active does not necessarily mean exercise. It is whatever active thing you're doing (as long as you're having fun), but exercises are certainly relaxing and a lot of fun.

Nature also helps everyone to be active. I have always loved the idea of nature. It had always been my go-to therapy whenever I felt like taking a break. The serene ambiance it radiates helps clear my mind and makes me more focused and peaceful. So, I have been hooked on the experience for a long time.

Yoga is one effective way to key into nature and experience the many benefits it has to offer. Simply laying your yoga mat and stretching in some relaxing poses can go a long way in restoring peace amidst the troubles and is also a good way of finding balance.

It doesn't matter if the yoga is done in your house or outside. Nature is everywhere. But it is also advisable to do exercises like taking walks to really experience nature in its rawest form.

One of our friendly neighbors is a doctor himself. He always says whatever your reason is, loss of a loved one or loss of a job or just loneliness, take a brisk walk. It will help you think, motivate you and change your perspective.

Little wonder just taking a walk can significantly lift your mood.

As much as sleeping is vital for the overall health, when done in excess, it can really lower productivity. Yet, people still resolve to sleep as the best way to avoid negativity. That only gives a temporary solution, except, of course, you want to sleep throughout the whole day for the rest of the year. Asides from the fact that that is technically not possible, where's the fun in that?

During the pandemic, my mom used to take my baby sister and me for a mile walk every evening. My baby sister and I used to collect flowers, leaves, and sometimes shiny stones and get those in Ziplock baggies on our way home. Once home, we used to wash them, play with them, and we used to make art with them too. It was fun.

In our case, by just walking, we had even done more than just that. We made art which is also a form of being active. All this we did while having fun.

Tennis and mini-golf are also my favorite sports (I know mini golf isn't a "real sport," but it's close enough, and besides, it's still really fun). An exciting golf match with family is also a way to breathe fresh air as well, as it is not super exhaustive, and you can play at your own pace. We stopped playing it altogether in 2020, but at the end of 2020, we started one on one matches, and we also went back to playing tennis and mini golf in certain areas. These sports have helped me make new friends and always helped me freshen up my mind, even during the pandemic.

Whatever the sports, whether primary or higher, ensure you are constantly being active as they will help you relax and have fun and is also an incredible way of improving your mental health.

For my 10th birthday in 2021, we did not throw any party. I just had my best friends over for a sleepover; we cut the cake and stayed indoors. Just a low-key celebration. But dad bought me a nice mountain bike and helmet. That was one of the coolest gifts I ever received. 🚲

I rode it every single day throughout the summer. I would hop on the bike and ride on our street sidewalk every day. On weekend mornings, my dad and I would go for 30 minutes biking around the neighborhood. In the end, we always stopped at a local donuts place and got kolaches and donuts. At the donut place, people had gotten so used to seeing our faces they would welcome us with happy smiles and ask, "the usual?" and I would go, "yes, please." I remember this one-time dad forgot his wallet, and he did not realize it until I had grabbed the donut bag off the counter. But the people were so lovely they said, "it's ok, it's on the house today," and gave us an order free that day. My dad thanked them. The next time we were there, he gave them a huge tip.

And it doesn't have to be a sport, walk, run, or gym workout. You can be active by just doing some yard work or by climbing stairs inside your house a few times. I recall me and my sister having a lot of fun every fall working with my dad in the backyard. First, we blow the leaves, wreck them, and then we get to jump in the leaves pile. Boy, the last part is always so much fun. My sister shows real potential for being a gymnast while we are on that last part.

So, here's a little advice, Workup, and most definitely, you will perk up!

3.

Say No to WiFi 📶

I know you might be wondering, 'Why to go off the internet when all I'm trying to do is have fun?'. I know it sounds boring, and trust me, I felt the same way at first.

The internet is now a part of our daily life, and it's hard to imagine going offline for a little bit, not to mention a few days. Just the thought of living without it makes you want to cry, and you think there's no way on Earth you can survive. It has become our 'savior,' an addiction of some sort because people believe it can help get them away from negativity and help them have fun. Of course, there's no denying that the internet is a fun place to be, whether it be playing online games, browsing, watching videos, or social media. Everything is just fun. However, we also can't deny that there is also negativity on the internet, except, of course, you want to focus on the positives only (which you should). Sometimes we don't intend for it, but we get absorbed in everything on the net, and the negativity somehow finds its way in.

But have you ever imagined yourself in a world without the internet? The things you would do if the concept of the internet never existed. How would you be spending your time?

I did not realize how much fun it was until I experienced it in Texas winter Freeze (January 2021).

Winter storms swept through the city, wreaking havoc on the city's energy infrastructure. In addition, it was bitterly cold outside. The roads were impassable, and there was a thick blanket of snow covering almost everything. Roads, roofs, backyards, and driveways were all covered in snow, and I believe it was the first time I had ever seen our driveway and backyard covered in snow. Due to the harsh weather, we were without power for two days, and our water supply was disrupted, among other things. So, we had no running water, no heat, and, of course, no Wi-Fi.

Luckily, my mom has this habit of storing water in bathtubs for every 'severe weather warning,' and we always have water bottles stocked up, so we had water. We bundled up in multilayered clothes, covered in blankets, and played board games as a family. We have a gas stove, so lighting it up with a birthday candle lighter was an experiment. We talked, laughed, cooked, cleaned, made art, and read books. We stayed current, listening to the radio in the car. I got to catch up on all the sudoku puzzles and kids' magazines.

This new improvement was so much fun that we decided to add a 'family's day off the grid' once every year. It was at that moment I realized that there was life outside the internet. And boy, was it more real and interesting. Let me tell you this, taking some time off the internet does more 'good' than you can imagine. It brings this peace and calm and even helps you spend more time physically with the people around you. Time spent disconnected can be where we find out more about ourselves and our families, as well as find inspirations, find motivations and even discover new things.

So, to try our first trip 'off the web' beginning of 2022, my dad booked a last-minute camping trip. The ranch was near the city but far enough to feel like a gateway. They had water, clean bathrooms, electricity, a playground with slides, a swing, and a lot of friendly pets there on the ranch. We played frisbee, and soccer, petted the farm animals and ran around catching chickens' the entire day. I got to read around the fire in the evening and finish some more sudoku. I speak for everyone when I say S'mores were the best part of a camping trip. We experimented quite a bit there with graham crackers, M&Ms, and PB&J flavors. All were so yum!

Our welcoming host also taught me how to meditate that evening. Until that point, I had never really grasped the concept of meditation. In a world where everything tends to be jumbled and sort of messed up, meditation is a way to focus the mind on one thing, blocking the rest out. It helps to really connect you with your inner self and can improve your overall well-being by reducing depression, anxiety, and pain.

Everyone can meditate, and here's how to do it. First, she told me to sit in a 'criss-cross applesauce position, close my eyes and rest my palms outward on my knees. Then I had to put my index finger to my thumb and just take big breaths in and out. That is especially supposed to help with peace and quiet for people of all ages. She also told me to practice this to deal with emotions; although I did not feel much difference at that moment, I plan to try that sometime later.

These days, most kids and adults are tied to at least one device most of the day, from social media to Netflix to online games and the likes. But we stayed away from electronics for an entire day. And to be honest, we did not miss it at all.

The next morning, we made breakfast from fresh eggs that the chickens laid and milk from the cows on the farm. I also got to see how they milk a cow by hand. And my first question to our lovely host was, "does that hurt a cow?" to my surprise, the answer was, "No, in fact, cows feel like a load off their chest," he said. Our host also offered us a trip to the milking parlor later that day. A milking parlor is a place where they milk a lot of their cows, more efficiently using pumps, multiple times a day. We made plans to go after lunch.

After we ate breakfast, we went off to play on the playground. Mom and dad were sitting on the patio drinking coffee and reading the newspaper. That is when my sister decided to play with potted plants. I think she wanted the pink rose but ended up grabbing the potted cactus before plucking the rose. A few seconds later, she had a bunch of tiny quills stuck in her fingers and immediately started crying.

It all happened so fast that we all noticed only when she started crying. Mom and dad came running. Picked her up. Mom got her phone (end of 'Off the grid' here), read a few tips online, called the host, and requested to get the tweezers and glue. It took them some time to find those, but they managed to get everything we needed. After a while, they had pulled all those quills out of my sister's hand, wiped them off, and then applied glue to her skin. Mom & dad decided to leave soon after that to see a doctor avoid further infection. So we cut short the rest of the trip and headed home. My sister seemed ok and slept most of the ride back home in the car. The trip surely did not end as we planned, but we did have a lot of fun during our day off the grid.

So, make a deliberate effort to take time off the internet and spend it doing something else. It could be exercising, walking, or spending it together with loved ones as we did.

Remember, it's just the internet.

4.

Youngling to the rescue

As cliche as it sounds, helping others goes a long way in making other people and even yourself happy. Helping others can come in different forms. One is volunteering, which is why my favorite happiness tip of all time is to Volunteer. It can be very satisfying. There are a lot of things you can achieve through volunteering. You can meet new people and make friends, achieve personal goals and be satisfied with yourself, hone a particular skill, and even discover new ones.

Volunteering is one fun way to get away from all the negativities. You get to escape from the daily routines, explore your interests, improve your social skills, energize yourself, and learn new things. And when you're done, you notice that you have contributed a lot and helped others. There are many fun volunteering opportunities, so find the right one for you and get started in helping others today.

Helping others can be as little as helping someone with the groceries bag, giving someone shelter, lending money to a friend, teaching someone how to do something, or even helping your mother with daily chores. Though these acts may seem little and inconsequential, they have a powerful effect on both parties. When you help others, you are not just putting a smile on their face; you are also putting a smile on their hearts which in turn creates happiness for you.

Today, where we live in a world of unending problems, we tend to get so occupied with ourselves forgetting how a simple act of kindness can brighten someone's day.

My city has seen its fair share of hurricanes. I remember when I was 7yrs old, we were hit by a big hurricane. This disaster caught the whole city off guard, and a lot of houses got flooded. Most of my friend's houses had their first floor flooded, and they had to climb up and stay on the second floor or, in some cases, in the attic.

One of my dad's coworkers had just had a baby and was in the hospital during that time. Their house and the way to the house were completely flooded. The hospital needed to vacate its rooms for emergency patients from other areas. They were offered shelter at the Town Conventional center, where most people were taking shelter during the flood. Parents with newborn babies were not very comfortable going to the convention center. So, my mom and dad offered them a room in our house, despite knowing the inconveniences they would pass through to get to the hospital.

Since most of the roads were flooded too, it was hard to find a way to and from the hospital. My dad had to go an extra mile to find a new route with low water areas, and even though it took much longer than usual, he managed to get the baby and parents to our home safely. They stayed with us for four days and then returned to their home once the water receded. They were so grateful to mom and dad and said thank you a bunch of times and invited us to their newly renovated house a few months later for a big party.

My mom and dad were in a position to help others, and they played their part in humanity.

The worst part of it was that one of my best friend's houses flooded both floors, and they had to be airlifted to rescue off their roof with his little brother. He and his family ended up moving out of the city too far away to another suburb after that hurricane. I was incredibly sad about his situation, and it touched something inside of me. That was the first time I felt the need to help people in need. I wanted to give back to the community, so if you are like me and want to give back to the community, here are a few fun ways to do that. Volunteering at your public library. When you do this, you are relieving the workers of stress because, more often than not, they are always overwhelmed with the work but never complain. And we see it as their responsibility, so we don't even bother to help. Imagine the smile on their faces when you volunteer to help them!

Another way is to teach people what you know how to do. Maybe you know how to dance or how to paint or are really good at any sports (football, running, etc.). You can volunteer to coach people and show them a lot of fun ways to use their talent.

You can volunteer to join a charity event like a yard sale, and the remittances can be used to buy clothes, books, and other stuff for people in the community who might be in need of them.

My favorite reason for volunteering is that when you help others, they are touched by your kindness, and this makes them also help other people. You are helping many other people you don't even know with a simple act of kindness.

When my school offered volunteers to sign up for local community projects, I signed up right away. I have done a couple of projects with school, and they were all fun. But my favorite one was volunteering for the biggest easter egg hunt in a local park. Lots of visitors showed up with babies and kids. We had egg hunts for kids of all ages; there were lots of fun activities. Kids were getting very creative with coloring and decorating foam eggs. Everyone enjoyed the fun stalls and food. Face painting and bunny cupcakes were the kid's favorites. The maple pecan latte was a major hit amongst the adults that day. People took lots of pictures with our easter bunny mascot. Local news reporters were there too, and they took a lot of pictures of everything and everyone. They even did a piece on us in the local magazine and newspaper. That felt very rewarding.

It felt very rewarding to see everyone happy, knowing that I was a small part of the reason for making it possible.

I really enjoy donating my time to a local soup kitchen as well. Everyone should try it once. Plus, you never know who you are going to run into and what new experiences you will gain from it. I remember we signed up to volunteer at a local food bank one time during the pandemic, and we had a local TV news anchor volunteering with us that shift. He was very friendly, and his personality was the same way, charming as we had seen on TV. He also helped me lift some of the heavy boxes that I was unable to move. Our shift was filled with laughter and hard work. I was the youngest on the team that day. So they gave me the nickname 'youngling,' just like in Star Wars.

I must agree there is only one thing more precious than our time, and that is what we spend it on. The best of us believe in spending our time doing good and making people smile. It is exciting and fun. Once you start volunteering, you will notice a change in your mood and others.

One other way to help others is to (and this is my mom's favorite) Clean up the house and donate any goodies you have lying around the house. Giving is also another form of helping. We do this twice a year, and the most fun part about this is that I end up finding a lot of stuff that I had been missing for a long time. I'd gather up all the old books, toys, games, clothes, bikes, etc. Then my sister and I end up playing with most of it for a few days all over again. After the whole thing is done, mom usually calls the Salvation Army to pick it up. But if you are interested in spending some more time, you can also sell it online or have a garage sale, then donate the money to your favorite charity. Helping others feels super gratifying. "In helping others, we shall help ourselves, for whatever good we give out completes the cycle and comes back to us."

So, no matter what happens, Volunteer to help, be kind, be a giver, and ensure to radiate positivity at all times. The universe definitely has a way of rewarding you!

5.

Sponsored by the plants!

My idea of green fun is helping to grow greens (such as plant-ing trees, flowers, fruit plants, vegetable plants, etc.) as much as possible. Here are some fun facts about trees. They have a positive impact on our health because being surrounded by trees helps us relax and reduce stress. They add beauty to the environment, especially the incredibly beautiful burst of color during fall. They give a sense of hope and rebirth as the leaves come blooming again. They can also serve as shade on a hot, sunny day. They provide food and shelter to animals (even the little creatures), so beautiful creatures like birds and all other fascinating animals take shelter in the trees. Even humans take shelter in trees (well, not in the way animals do); from trees, we get timber which is used for human shelter and a whole lot of other things.

Planting a tree is like birthing a new life. You get to take care of it, water it and add all the necessary things for it to grow. And trust me, every single part of this process is fun. Watching them grow brings much excitement. Planting trees also means you are contributing positively to the Earth; let's not forget climate change and how disastrous it can be. At the end of it all, when the tree has matured, you look at it with satisfaction and say, 'I did that.'

Trees are more than just trees. Flowering trees even offer extra benefits because of their flowers. You get to see a lot of butterflies in your yard. You get to experience the sweet smell, and the air around feels very different. You even get to pick out special flowers as gifts to your loved ones on special occasions, whether Valentine's Day, Mother's Day, Father's Day, birthdays, or even teacher's day.

Flowers can help you put a smile on people's faces and yours too.

It may not sound very intriguing, but planting trees is a fun activity that almost every child will remember. So, hear my experience out and give it a try.

My first experience with plants was when I planted a tree, which was when we moved into our new house, which had a big empty backyard. A couple of weeks after we moved in, my dad spoke with someone from the county office as he made some marks in our front and backyard. I think they told him the exact safe locations to dig around the house to plant trees. In the afternoon, we went to the nearest garden center and bought an orange, lemon, birch, and some Texas red oak plants, along with all the other supplies we would need to help plant them. Dad pretty much taught me everything I needed to know.

I wore the smallest available gloves that were still a bit bigger on my hands, and we started with the backyard. We dug the holes first. Then we loosened the roots, removed the plastic, and put the plants in the holes. After filling up the soil, we staked the plants and supported them with ties. Mulching and watering came at the end. Oaktree plants went in the front, close to the end of our driveway. I absolutely loved the whole experience. Playing with water and soil, in general, is so much fun and will make you happy.

After we planted everything, dad had to take care of the plants every day. We would walk around the house, water them, fix the support if needed, and check on their growth.

Our birch tree and red oaks have grown a whole lot bigger over the years. They cast a perfect shade in our backyard and driveway for us to play under. They cool the place down in summer. The birch tree turns bright yellow and sheds all its leaves every fall; it looks so beautiful. I also get to pick lots of lemons every year in summer to make lemonade. We also enjoy super sweet, ripe oranges every November during thanksgiving break.

My whole experience with this was so surprisingly happy that I decided to plant something on my own during pandemic summer break. I picked a couple of rose and chili plants from the local gardening center with my mom's help. I followed all the steps dad had taught me along with my sister. Did I mention she had the time of her life there? Soil and water were all over her that day. She made pretend food (pancakes, donuts, cupcakes, etc.) from soil and dirt and set up her restaurant with a menu, prices, and everything. We laughed so hard. We ended up putting our rose plants a couple of feet apart from each other and buried the chilies in the soft soil. Mom was not very happy about the clothes and dirt, but she got over it.

After coming inside, I set up an alarm to water my plants every day. By the end of the summer, my chilies and rose plants were all grown about 3 feet tall. We got a lot of chilies and roses that summer. Most of the chili plants froze during the Texas freeze. Next winter, however, big ones like birch and oak trees, most of the roses, and the orange and lemon plants grew back and were blooming again. That taught me to believe in a new tomorrow. I also use the roses we get to put a bouquet together for Teacher's Day and Mother's Day.

I am planning to continue this fun adventure. This year on Earth Day, we went to the new park that was getting built in our neighborhood and helped plant a small oak tree there. I can't wait to see it grow.

Planting trees is fun, and there are a lot of experiences attached to it.

6.

Business is booming $$$

Entrepreneurship can be explained in so many ways. First, it is a way of learning new skills through experience. It involves brainstorming new ideas, showing these ideas to the world, selling to interested persons, and making some nice profits.

It may sound more math than fun, but what if I told you that entrepreneurship is getting to try something new, learning and improving with friends or even yourself, meeting new people in the process, and making a huge profit?

We all know the story of the well-known entrepreneur Walt Disney.

Yes, Walt Disney did, in fact, grow up on a farm drawing cartoon characters and continued to do so as an adult. (This was his idea.) He eventually landed a job in a movie company and created a cartoon character for them. (He sold his idea/rendered his service to the movie company.) However, when the company decided to reduce his pay, he quit his job. He created another cartoon character, this time for himself, and found recognition for it- I know we're all familiar with Mickey Mouse, the all-time kids' favorite (He started to make some nice profit)

This is also to tell you that entrepreneurship does not necessarily mean buying and selling. It could also be rendering of services. And I bet you Walt Disney had fun in creating those cartoon characters. Because of him and his cartoons, many people around the world are happy.

I could go on and on and give you names of entrepreneurs and their exciting stories from Oprah Winfrey, Walt Disney, Madame CJ Walker, and Steve Jobs.

Steve Jobs transformed his idea into a company by taking a risk. He created the now-famous Apple products.

Not so boring anymore now, huh?

I'm sure you are now fully interested in hearing about my fun experiences in Entrepreneurship. So, let's get started.

Over the summer/winter vacation, my parents usually sign me up for camps of my choice. I had done a Leadership Entrepreneurship skills camp last winter and wanted to take a stab at it. Being an entrepreneur is about finding a way to combine resources. It involves taking risks. Over the summer, I pitched the idea to my friends during one sleepover, and they were all thrilled to start our business venture. The first step was coming up with an interesting idea for retail arbitrage.

Our main goal was to get our feet wet and earn some money (if we could). We all did some research from all available resources. We listed down all the places where we can buy our high-quality supplies for the lowest possible price. Next, we started gathering our money from our piggy bank savings. A few of us took small neighborhood jobs like babysitting, dog walking, and lawn mowing to earn extra cash. We ended up buying 'off season' kid's clothes from Target, Walmart, Kohls, eBay, and Local garage sales and stocked them in a small room inside my house under the stairs.

e.g., winter coats, jackets, and sweaters were cheap at the beginning of spring. So the next step was to work on putting our blog and list down all our inventory online for sale.

We had to improvise as we progressed and learned a few new skills like advertising on social media sites. We also had to get the hang of digital marketing. It took some time, but we started getting orders by the end of summer. I remember when we had our first order, my friend called me at night. It was after 9 pm when I was about to sleep, and he almost screamed with excitement that we had our first order. I fell asleep with extra confidence that night planning the shipping. Over the time, we got tons of orders and had to work hard that fall to keep up the inventory and pack and ship orders. We delivered nearby orders with the help of our older teenage friends who could drive. I was the youngest on the team.

I remember this one-time when a friend tripped in the storage area. The box he was carrying slipped and fell on other boxes, causing the entire inventory to scatter across the room.

Luckily, he did not get hurt and was just bruised. Another friend who was working nearby was also bruised as one box hit his shoulder before landing on the floor. We ended up putting frozen peas on their bruises. All of us helped to put the inventory back in its place a little later after the incident. In hindsight, it does not seem like a big deal, but it was a significant learning experience for all of us. We all handled it with good maturity and leadership qualities and are proud of ourselves.

We continued for about a year and decided to split the profit equally. After that, we got the zest for hunting marketplaces, managing the blog, digital marketing, and inventory maintenance.

It doesn't have to be big. It could be a lemonade stand, a yard sale, or even a fundraiser for charity. Either way, as long as it's something that teaches you about financial stuff like savings, and spending, it will give you business experience. I plan to pursue my entrepreneur dreams in the future as well. So, I hope you will give it a try and have some fun along the way.

7.

Don't you dare mention work 🏖

Taking a vacation is an exciting experience, especially when it involves traveling to a new place. You get to experience the culture, new food, sights, and all other beautiful experiences that come with a changing environment. Ok, now I know 'taking a vacation is not something kids can control. But we all know how taking a vacation helps everybody in the family to relax, spend quality time with each other, to rejuvenate, and get back in the game more focused than ever. So, you can help your parents plan your next Vacation.

There's just something about Vacation that even the mere thought of planning it gets you extremely excited. Yes, you don't have to wait until you arrive at your destination to have fun. Instead, you can start having fun during the pre-trip activities. Activities like composing your list, researching the place, writing down interesting places you want to visit, and even packing.

Organizing a list of items you want to take along will help you remember to pack everything you need to enjoy your experience. Researching the place will help prepare your mind for the things you'd meet there, which eases you into the environment beforehand. And when you eventually get there, you will find yourself having so much fun. The thrill and excitement that comes with writing down places you want to visit are inexplicable (I'm not exaggerating, I promise). Your brain is already anticipating those places, and you are so energized that even if the trip is not until the following week, you keep walking around the house in a fun and exciting mood.

So, if you've not been trying pre-trip activities like this, you should definitely give it a try on your next Vacation.

Another interesting part about Vacation is the feeling that accompanies it. That special elevated mood that everyone is in a few weeks before and even after. It doesn't matter whether it's a long drive in your car or flying to another state or country. The shopping, packing, planning, flying, food, all of it; is a multitude of exciting things about a vacation that brings all members together. It not only perks up everyone's interests and ideas but also gives everyone a break from the regular cycle of life. It adds to the list of memories and, not to mention, improves overall health.

Frequent or even seldom trips like these come together, and before you know it, a particular one has been etched into memory as your favorite. I know I cannot be the only one that has that one special memory of a particular trip or Vacation etched into my brain as my favorite. But, here's the good part, we still keep making more and adding new ones to the list.

So, yes, I'm always a little too excited (maybe not a little, but) when it comes to taking a break and exploring the beauty of other places. And that is what Vacation gives- an opportunity to explore. And don't forget, exploring is fun!

One of my favorite memories of ours would be when we traveled to Singapore one summer. We had a list of all the important things to take. I recall us having a separate big list of electronics itself to pack—universal power adapters, portable chargers, headphones, cameras, e-readers, and earplugs, to name a few. Luckily, we all packed for ourselves and reminded each other what we packed, so we did not miss anything. The city's unique structure is one thing to gawk at. They have excellent public transportation in Singapore, which makes it easier to enjoy the city's unique fusion of modern architecture with traditional Asian allure. Me and my baby sister loved the closeness to wildlife during night safari. I love how the new place feels different, and you hear noises while trying to sleep. I sure do miss my bed on such occasions. I did not know the drums I kept hearing early morning were from the Buddha Tooth Relic temple until we visited it.

Taking a vacation helps you experience the true beauty of humanity. You get to see diverse other people and how they act, interact with new people and make amazing new friends. When we were at Sentosa Island taking the fort tour, my mom got a phone call about her bank card. I think it was from the local Singapore branch, and they were telling my mom to come to pick up her card with an ID that she was missing. Funny enough, mom did not notice that she was missing the card until she got the call. She quickly realized she may have left it in China town the previous day during all the hustle and excitement. After the tour, we were able to locate the bank branch and pick it up. Mom did not want to cancel the card because she was using it for autopay at multiple places, and she was able to see no fraud. We all were amazed by the honesty and efforts of the locals to get it back to her too.

Taking a vacation also brings challenges because you are away from your normal life. Sometimes it is quite tasking to adapt to a new lifestyle which is why I like to do proper research about the place we are making a trip to. Study the language (if you can), learn about the culture, and, if possible, take virtual tours. All these should be done during the pre-trip stage so that you can make the most fun out of it. But these challenges also have their good side because while trying to adapt, you develop new skills or techniques. It helps you to adjust your attitude to twist things for good results. Every time we are on a break, I develop a new capability that I never knew I had.

I remember when we were shopping in Nassau, Bahamas straw market, my dad gave me control of bargaining for the handcrafted wooden lionfish I wanted. It was exciting how the local sellers were treating me like a prince. The seller said to me in his Bahamian English accent, "I will give you this for $60. Only for you, my blue-eyed prince. Because I want to see your charming smile and remember me when you go home by the lionfish." His words made me smile, made me happy, and I was excitingly surprised when the price came down to almost half of what they initially labeled.

Travel also teaches you a lot of different things like reading a map, history, navigating through a new place, and understanding the language in the local accent. It can even expand your appetite for new food. You will develop those new taste buds.

I will never forget the taste of 'switcha,' the famous Bahamian lemonade.

We all like to venture out to new restaurants, especially while traveling. So, I decided to try conch fritters in Nassau's famous fish fry restaurant. I have also learned from previous travel experiences that 'no question is silly when you are not home. So, I did ask the server for details about the dish. The first thing I learned was that I was mispronouncing it. It is pronounced as "Konk" but spelled as a conch. Then upon finding out that conch is a sea snail from local Caribbean waters. I was a little skeptical about trying. However, our friendly waiter told me, "It is really good." I am telling you; I am glad I trusted him.

It was so tasty that I had conch fritters pretty much every day while in the Bahamas. I decided that day I was going to give different food and flavors at least one non-biased try. It's true, never a dull moment when you are on Vacation.

Travel helps me understand different cultures, religions, and ways of life that I do not see on my routine days. It basically increases my cultural understanding, and I can empathize more with the locals. I have so many memorable moments from my trips so far skydiving, parasailing, jet-skiing, scuba diving. All these skills I have learned, and the thrills I have had are hard to forget. Sometimes it is even fun when you just randomly remember some of these exciting moments. I cherish those memories. I also collect small flags and coins from all the places we visit.

I must admit, though, I love my home a lot more at the end of each Vacation. I love that nostalgic feeling of coming home from a vacation. I think it's true that "life can be very boring only for dull people, so don't wait, make yours interesting, go traveling and be happy."

8.

Books, Books, and more books 📚

In today's age, where the internet has taken over, the pleasure derived from reading books can be so underrated. Reading takes us out of our normal routine of staring at the screen all day. It is an excellent way to relax and immerse yourself in an entirely different world, and this right here is bliss!

It also helps broaden our knowledge, improve vocabulary, improve skills, and energize our minds. Through reading, we can learn different things, and even the most complicated things can be broken down and easily understood. So, it is like a win-win situation; you have fun and at the same time get a truckload of other benefits.

You can read different things and for many reasons. Some people derive fun in reading newspapers (our parents and grandparents for sure), and some derive fun in reading comics. I know a few friends that love comics. Some in magazines, sports, even manuals, and some derive pleasure in reading stories, including me.

That's right, and I derive absolute fun in reading stories.

It could be bedtime stories, anime stories, fairy tale stories, or whatever genre you are interested in reading.

Reading is Fun. Not just for yourself but reading to others can be very joyous too. You could read for your friends, siblings, parents, and even grandparents as long as they are willing to listen. In my own case, I first started to read to my baby sister during the pandemic, and boy, at first, it wasn't easy.

If you have a younger sibling (especially toddlers) at home, you will know what I mean. Reading to them is an amazing experience, but at first, it could be tiring because they most probably will not pay attention. And they are the loudest humans.

My sister was two years old when I started reading to her during the pandemic. She was loud and never really paid attention, mostly because she had just begun to figure out talking, singing, making new words, etc. Whenever I read to her, she mostly just blabbered away and ignored me. Oh my god, that girl can talk. I mean so much! As if that was not enough, crying was also one of her favorite things to do, especially if she did not get her way. And when I say crying, I mean full-on crying with tears and everything. My sister can be adorable until she is not. But I found a fantastic way to calm her down, divert her attention, and read to her.

It wasn't easy at first. I used to sit next to my baby sister, where she would play with her dollhouse, and I would start reading. For many days, in the beginning, she would just ignore me. She wouldn't even look at the book and just move on playing with her new toys, run away, start talking to her toys, anything but reading. I felt so bad. But I kept going, mainly because mom used to pay me an allowance.

Reading to others is not so much fun until your story sparks the interest of the listener, and they start paying attention.

After a couple of weeks, I noticed she started showing interest and started holding books (upside down at first). ☺

Then she started copying me, making her own stories, and looking at the pictures. That is when I realized she was listening. A few more days later, she would say a couple of words from our routine, repetitions of the same stories. And then sometimes she started requesting it. For example, "Can we weed beauty and beast' stowy today?" or "Can we weed Cindwella today?". It was honestly very rewarding.

Overall, the whole reading process was fun and tiring at first but definitely worth it at the end of the day. Reading for your siblings or a loved one can also motivate you to spread happiness and read to other people.

Now my sister sits close to me and loves reading and listening to stories. We enjoy reading together, and I have discovered my storytelling skills with her. It also inspired me to read for other toddlers at a local library. I have attended a few storytime events as a kid myself, and I always wanted to lead one too. I was very happy when I was picked as the reader over the last winter break; I got to pick my stories to read (which was a good thing because I had a lot of practice). I knew very well to express the characters with my tone. It was so encouraging to watch my audience and allow them to imagine what was going on. Their faces lit up with a smile at every joke. I had a super good time.

There are a plethora of ways in which reading can make you happy. Reading can help you discover some flaws you didn't know you had and help you improve on them. We all know how fun improving ourselves can be. You wake up every day excited to discover what the day holds in store for you, excited to find out about new things that could potentially help you.

Reading has inspired a writer inside me as well. So often, we forget the "W's" about the books we read, which, what, when, where, etc. I often try to remember to myself what I read and struggle to remember. So, I like to make notes about the book. I write in my daily journal. Sometimes, I write my unity game scripts using it too.

9.

Small call for a big win! 📱

While most people think that technology isn't good for you. I would say it's good for you if you use it properly that is. Stuff like making calls to family members or friends, which is most definitely a need and not a want. When you make a call to friends or even loved ones you probably have not seen in a while, there is that feeling of happiness you get, and you just know that chatting could not have done it like that.

Simply putting a call through could help make you feel better in many ways. It can help you relax since you get to hear their voice and sometimes even the emotions in their voice. It makes you feel closer to the person even though they are miles away.

A word of advice from people you value at your down moments can really change your whole mood. Friends also get to share their own experiences with you. You get to hear about their own side of the world, how they're faring all the while making silly jokes and laughing together like they're right in front of you.

I used to wait for school closures & holidays like crazy. We used to jump up and down, waiting to see if school closures were announced last minute due to some weather issues or so. I never thought I would ever say the words "I miss school; I miss my friends." But during those virtual schooling days of the pandemic, I seriously missed school and all my friends.

I struggled to get in touch with my buddies. I wanted to tell them many things, play games, etc., but I was bored. Finally, my mom ended up texting a couple of my friend's moms to get us connected. We all set up discord and established a routine to get together online during a certain time every day, and we would chat, play games, and tell jokes. It was so relaxing. I didn't realize how many roles making a call played in lifting my mood until then.

We still do that, and I stay connected with my friends even on holidays and weekends, no matter where they are. This is especially helpful during summer when most of my friends are traveling somewhere.

We have all lost a lot of everyday interactions during the pandemic, and as I'm sure you know, isolation can lead to stress and negativity. I believe it is important that we all socialize to some degree. Socialization is also very good for our mental and emotional well-being. Admittedly, you have your immediate family to keep you company, but we can't deny half the time, we also want to interact with our friends and other distant people.

The good thing is that your family and friends are all closer than ever with the technology. Remember putting a call through to a loved one doesn't just make you happy. It makes them happy too.

Never be too shy to make a call. WhatsApp, Discord, Zoom, Teams, Facetime, etc. There are so many options for calling these days. I just feel it is easier to communicate on calls; your tone and expressions can convey a lot more than a text or chat message of a few words.

So, I always prefer to stay in touch with my friends & distant family on a communication app. I speak with my uncle, aunt's cousins, and my super favorite Grandpa and grandma at least once a week. Grandma and Grandpa are always happy to listen to me. We talk about a lot of things; I show them the games I made, short dance videos I made, my school projects, my new toys, and new books. They always make me happy and value me tremendously. They listen to whatever I have to say or complain about and give me loads of valuable advice, sometimes gifts too. They are my one stop to share anything and everything. My Grandpa has taught me this funny way of expressing emotions in all kinds of situations. It is called fill-in-the-blanks. It is a way to use your words to describe that emotion at that moment instead of getting bummed about it. e.g., After I hung up the call with my grandparents, I looked at my sister and asked her, "I love grandma and grandpa! Talking to them makes me very …." and since she has to fill in the blank with one-word emotion, she goes "Happy."

This is one of the best ways to convey that emotion to some level as long as the message is understood. This is also proof that a call can make you develop new and interesting ways of talking to each other.

They say a word is enough for the wise' and it's true. Mom and Dad usually don't scold or ground us. Just fill in the blank of this emotion. My sister has learned all sorts of emotional words by filling in the blanks every day. She has taken upon herself this responsibility very seriously, to personally experiment and try out all fill-in-the-blanks. You name it, and she has worked on it. Sad, mad, happy, angry, proud, stressed, worried, scared, tired, cool, excited, annoyed, goofy, silly. She has all the emojis learned in her head (most of them, probably with my mom's face on them) without seeing actual emojis. I think there is a scientific reason behind it too. I read it once, expressing your emotion in words and dialing down the immediate reaction to it. So, it is a 'Win-Win' for both parents and kids.

10.

Never be bored again!

There is a lot of fun in being creative, whether it is solitary, with a sibling, or even in the community. Community-driven creatives like cheerleading, music bands, Art classes, and the likes help to bring people together.

Being creative is easing your mind of bothersome thoughts while still engaging your mind and deriving pleasure.

Creativity is a way to freely express your thoughts and emotions by bringing new ideas into reality.

And here's the good part, you don't have to be an expert to experience the fun that creativity brings. Likewise, you don't need to have all the knowledge in the world before you can be creative. It can be as little as painting the walls, setting up makeshift tents in the house, combining dresses to come up with a unique style, or even cutting pieces of cardboard to form different structures.

Creativity doesn't always involve spending long hours. But just forty minutes away from your routine, doing something you like can help make you happy. It helps you relax, and you are at peace with yourself, forgetting every noise and problem. There is also a feeling of satisfaction and inner happiness when you look at what you've created. It works just like magic and is a lot of fun.

Creativity can also make people around you happy. A good example is video games. All video games we play are someone's creativity, and I'm sure you know how much of a smile plays on people's faces when they grab the pad to play.

Being creative means, you're creating something new, and it can come in a lot of forms. Like making arts or drawing, baking, doing a puzzle, inventing things, solving basic problems, writing a book, telling a story in a different kind of way, coming up with new methods to things, etc.

My favorite creativity options are creating games and creating video projects. You do not have to be good at it. You just have to get good with it over time.

My Grandpa gifted me a canon power shot camera last Christmas to flare my interest in filming. It has worked. I take it with me on every trip outdoors. I have captured a lot of fun, memorable family moments so far. My sister is learning to ride her scooter, mastering her ramp walk on TikTok music, and trying oysters for the first time, just to name a few.

My very first exciting experience of filming was not too long ago. We were in Destin, Florida, on spring break. We were traveling with one of our family friends, and all had rented a local two-story house via Airbnb. House was airy and beautiful. We were surrounded by a few houses down the street. It had an excellent view of palm trees and the beach from our balcony.

One morning I had my camera out in one hand and was trying to sip my OJ on the terrace. I was mainly focused on capturing the seashore waves. Little did I know the real treasure was closer in the view. When I moved the focus a bit close to the street area, I saw a big black lump with a long narrowing end. I realized it was a gigantic gator, more like a live speed bump, within a fraction of seconds. It was bigger than our SUV and was not moving at all at the time. After we all got a good view that quiet morning, my dad alerted local authorities; while he was on the phone, the gator started his morning walk, flapping his long tail, and went on his way.

When I sent that video to my family members, a bunch of wide-mouth, shocking LOL emojis came flying my way. My Grandpa expressed his feelings of awe and happy surprise over the phone call and even shared the video with all his friends.

We often laugh a lot looking at some of the old videos my parents and I took. Everyone has their way of expressing creative thoughts. My sister has her way too. She paints. And I mean everything, including our walls, sometimes with peanut butter and jelly handprints.

We used her Nutella chocolate handprint to make turkey art on paper. We are proud of ourselves and have hung it in my room. She also loves dressing up in new fashion. We tried making a new dress for her from plastic bags; we used 2-sided tape to stitch it together one weekend. We had fun with that. One time we just wrapped her around with paper towels and made her a Halloween mummy costume.

There is fun even in the most seemingly inconsequential things, and all it takes is a positive mind to see it. Little gestures can make people's day, a little idea can motivate you, one phone call can lift your mood, a simple walk can refix your thoughts, a simple vacation can change your perspective, taking time off can help you realize the little things, and simply ignoring some things can bring so much peace.

Most times, we are so buried in the negativity around us that we fail to see that it doesn't take a whole lot to be happy. So have fun with the things that make you happy.

"Be simple, be Happy" that's my motto because when you're happy, you positively influence the things around you. You Spread positivity!

Remember, life always has ups and downs, but you can stay happy through it all.

Now my friends, there you have it. I have revealed the secret tips for staying happy and having fun even when things don't seem to be going smoothly. I hope you enjoyed reading my tips and experiences.

But hey, before you go, there is one last secret. I never told you my first name or my sisters. But before I reveal to you our real names, know that she goes by 'Queen.' Yes, she calls herself a Queen. When I first asked her, "Do you mean 'princess?!'" She said, "No, thank you, I prefer to be the Queen." Indeed, she is the queen of the family in general, and between you and me, the most annoying one too.

But Shhhh…we are Joy and Jolly. Literally, I am the "Joy," and she is the "Jolly."

ACKNOWLEDGMENTS

I would like to thank to all my mentors and teachers for being with me every step of the way.

A special thanks to my parents and grandparents for allowing me to take creative risks and supporting my dreams.

I am grateful to all my friends' editors, illustrators, and all of you who volunteered to read and help me make my first book.

Writing this book seemed impossible at times and would not have happened without constant support from you all. A huge thank you to everyone who encouraged me and told me I can make it happen.

I appreciate you all.

—Vivaan Sadare

ABOUT THE AUTHOR

Vivaan Sadare is 11 yrs. Old. He likes to write short stories, quotes, and code. Vivaan often tries to find joy in simple things and be creative with them. He strongly believes in taking baby steps to achieve bigger things. He enjoys biking, playing tennis, creating video games, and having sleepovers with his friends.

Vivaan's short stories are bought to life in this book with fictitious characters and eye-catching illustrations. Reading them will put you in a great mood. The book's main idea is to give inspiration, a boost of creativity and perhaps a chance of hope.

Researchers have shown a significant connection between kids' healthy self-esteem and its positive effects. A1Day Stories' is one of the easiest ways to gain that much-needed passion and high self-esteem.

So, read along and pass along.